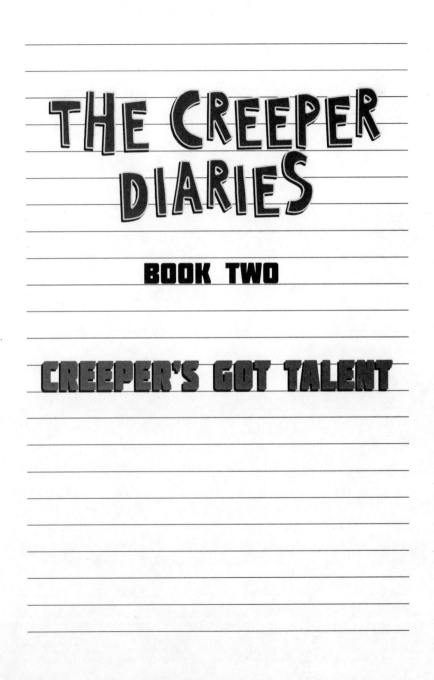

THE CREEPER DIARIES

BOOK TWO

CREEPER'S GOT TALENT

THE CREEPER DIARIES

BOOK TWO

CREEPER'S GOT TALENT

GREYSON MANN

ILLUSTRATED BY AMANDA BRACK

Sky Pony Press
New York

Sky Pony Press books may be purchased in bulk at special discounts for sales promotion, corporate gifts, fund-raising, or educational purposes. Special editions can also be created to specifications. For details, contact the Special Sales Department, Sky Pony Press, 307 West 36th Street, 11th Floor, New York, NY 10018 or info@skyhorsepublishing.com.

Visit our website at www.skyponypress.com.

10 9 8 7 6 5 4 3 2 1

Library of Congress Cataloging-in-Publication Data is available on file.

Special thanks to Erin L. Falligant.

Cover illustration by Amanda Brack
Cover design by Brian Peterson

Hardcover ISBN: 978-1-5107-1821-0
Ebook ISBN: 978-1-5107-1830-2

Printed in the United States of America

DAY 1: TUESDAY (MORNING)

I was just a kid when I started Mob Middle School a month ago. I've gotta say, I've grown a lot since then.

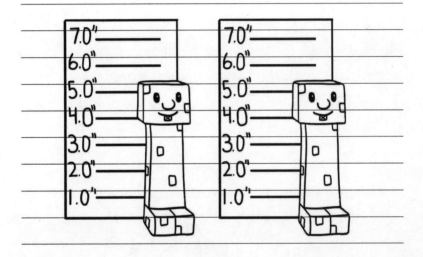

I somehow made it through the first month in one piece. Well, EXCEPT for the day I exploded in the cafeteria, taking out the vending machine and a bully named Bones. But that's another story.

See, I had all these dreams when school started. I thought I could give myself this cool new nickname, and make friends with an Enderman, and be the fastest creeper in sprinting class.

Well, things didn't go exactly how I thought they would. I might have dreamed a little TOO big. But I still think a creeper should have a plan.

My real dream plan is to be a famous rapper someday, like Kid Z. I'm only in sixth grade now, so I've got like six years to make that happen. I think that's pretty realistic.

Meanwhile, I've got a shot at being a famous rapper RIGHT HERE at Mob Middle School. These fliers were posted all over school last night talking about a talent show. It's a month from now.

That seems like a long way away, but it gives me plenty of time to plan.

I can picture it already: me on stage, rapping, with mobs falling at my feet. All those eighth-grade witches will be BEGGING for my autograph.

That's where everything kind of falls apart, because no one knows my real name. It's Gerald, which is a weird name for a creeper. I tried to change it when I started school, but that plan backfired and kids started calling me Itchy. (Don't ask—it's a long story.)

So I'm trying to turn moldy mushrooms into mushroom stew. That's what Mom says we should do with bad situations—find a way to make something good out of them. So if I can't lose my new nickname, I gotta find a way to make it cool.

I think the talent show could help me out there. If I win, everyone will want something signed by Itchy. They'll be making T-shirts with my name on them and everything!

The way I see it, only TWO things stand in my way of winning.

The first one is Bones and his gang. That skeleton has pretty much left me alone the last couple of days—you know, after the blowing-up-in-his-face incident. But I overheard him say to his buddies that they should enter their band in the talent show.

I didn't know Bones even HAD a band. I didn't think that nasty skeleton had a musical bone in his body.

But if he does, he'll be hard to beat. When he decides to do something (like make my life miserable), he's pretty good at making it happen.

Here's the second thing that might stand in my way of winning the show. It's possible that I MIGHT have a teeny-tiny problem with stage fright.

I wasn't worried about that at first, because I figured my friend Sam and I would do the act together. Having that big, bouncy slime onstage with me would make things a whole lot better.

So, at lunchtime, I met Sam in the cafeteria by the new vending machine. I have to say, I kind of did the school a favor by blowing up the old one. This new machine ALWAYS takes my emeralds, and food actually comes out instead of getting stuck.

Sam likes the new machine because it has hot chocolate. I guess it's made from cocoa that comes all the way from the jungle. But anyway, Sam can't get enough of it. And let me just say, that slime does NOT need caffeine. He's bouncy enough. And when he has caffeine, he wiggles constantly.

But now he's kind of addicted. So while he got his hot chocolate, I asked him about the talent show. Turns out, he's already doing an act with his girlfriend, Willow.

Personally, I don't think a sixth-grade slime should be going out with an eighth-grade witch. But I learned a long time ago (last month) not to get involved. I do NOT need that kind of drama in my life.

So I guess Willow Witch is doing some kind of potion-brewing act, and Sam is going to be her assistant. I don't really get it. Why would a slime want to be a witch's assistant when he could be a creeper's backup musician?

But, whatever. I guess I'm on my own.

So when I got home after school this morning, I talked to Mom about it. Well, I had to wait until she was done working out first.

Mom is on this fitness kick. Last month, it was an "eat green foods" kick, so this is a definite improvement—at least, for me.

The green-foods thing was an epic fail. Mom was trying to look younger and greener, but that didn't really happen. Plus, Mom found out that Dad was sneaking dinners at the Creeper Café.

He just couldn't take any more brussels sprouts.

I couldn't either. Like I told Mom once, I blame those brussels sprouts for my blow-up at school. But she doesn't really want to discuss that anymore. She says it's time to move on.

So when Mom finished her workout DVD, I told her about the talent show.

BIG MISTAKE.

She said I should ask my twin sister, Chloe, to be my partner in the show. See, Mom has all these hopes and dreams for Chloe and me, now that we're not fighting all the time.

I used to call her my Evil Twin. But Chloe has actually been nice to me lately because I saved her butt at school last week. I gotta say, though, I don't see us being BFFs anytime soon. And trying to do a talent show act with her would be a COMPLETE disaster. So Mom really has to start being more realistic.

Anyway, I told Mom I'd figure it out on my own. I have a whole month, and I just need to make a plan.

The first thing I have to do is finish my new rap. I started over the weekend, but I haven't worked on it since. See, I'm doing this sprinting thing after school, and that extracurricular is really cramping my style.

Turns out, sprinting is NOT my talent. I tried practicing in the backyard once. But, for some reason, that didn't really improve my speed. And I haven't been able to talk Sam into joining sprinting. So it's just me and Ziggy Zombie.

The only thing worse than having to run for an hour is running with a zombie chasing you. And the other day, Ziggy actually caught up with me. I'm afraid he might pass me pretty soon. And when a ZOMBIE is a faster runner than you, it's DEFINITELY time to quit.

Dad won't want me to quit sprinting. He's big on sticking with what you started. But I think Mom will help me out there—especially when I bring up the fact that she quit the "going green" thing. (Parents really love it when you bring up examples to back up your argument.)

So I think I have a good plan going. Here's what I've got so far:

30-Day Plan for Winning the Talent Show
- Find a partner—or another way to lose my stage fright. (Is there a potion for that?)
- Quit sprinting class.
- Finish writing my rap song.

I think that's a pretty realistic plan. And I'm going to start right away.

At dinner, I'll ask Mom and Dad about quitting sprinting. It's always good to do these things after parents have had a good day's sleep.

Like I said, a month ago, I was just a kid with big dreams. But I'm a whole lot smarter now. I'm a creeper with a plan.

DAY 1: TUESDAY (NIGHT)

Well, dinner was pretty much a disaster.

I mean, the eating part was good. Scorched salmon, roasted potatoes, and not a single green thing on my plate. But everything tasted so good that I didn't want to ruin it by talking about sprinting class. So I waited until dessert.

As soon as Mom brought out the burnt apple crisp, I made my big announcement. I said I was quitting sprinting class because I had to focus on my career as a rap artist. Dad opened his mouth just like I knew he would, so I quickly passed him the apple crisp and served him up a big heaping.

Then I pulled out my secret weapon. I said, "I really think a creeper should know when to quit. Take Mom here, for example. When that whole brussels sprout thing didn't pan out, she decided to throw it out the window and move on. Right, Mom?"

I was pretty proud of the way I'd just taken Dad's attention off me and put it on Mom. But, boy, did THAT backfire.

Before I could even take one bite of my burnt apple crisp, Mom slid my plate away and put her green face right in front of mine.

She said, "For your information, I didn't QUIT the brussels sprout thing. I replaced my plan to eat green with my new and improved plan to become an exercise machine. Which happens to be going very well, thanks for asking. I've already lost three pounds of gunpowder. You should ALL try it. In fact, I think we should start jogging as a family. Every night before dinner."

"Hey, there's an idea!" said Dad. "Gerald can run with you!"

I don't know how "family" turned into "Gerald," but I guess Dad thought I should take one for the team.

Right away, I asked why my sisters weren't part of this family-jogging plan. But I wished I hadn't said that, because it reminded Mom about the talent show. And she got in my face again and asked if I'd invited Chloe to be my partner in the show.

I played dumb and pretended she was talking about one of my OTHER sisters. Did I mention I have three?

"Isn't Cate a little too old?" I said.

My teenaged sister, the Fashion Queen, glared at me. Cate hasn't had much of a sense of humor since Dad said she couldn't date this guy named Steve. She's been wearing a black wig and dark lipstick and moping around the house.

It's kind of bringing me down, actually. I almost wish Dad would let her and Steve hiss and make up.

So then Mom was like, "Not THAT sister."

So I said, "Oh, you mean Cammy?"

My baby sister, Cammy, is talented, all right. I call her the Exploding Baby because she blows up ALL the time. She could be my partner in the talent show if I could just get her to explode on cue—like right at the end of my rap song.

"Bringing down the house, yo,
with all this gloom and doom,
Bringing down the house
With a crazy baby...
BOOM!"

For half a second, I actually considered it.

But Mom had zero patience left by then. She used my whole name, which is never a good sign. "You're not funny, Gerald Creeper, Jr. You know perfectly well that I'm talking about Chloe."

Chloe looked up from the burnt apple crisp that she'd been inhaling. She had a big chunk of charred apple stuck to her cheek. I wondered if anyone was going to mention it.

When she said she was already working on her own act—something about a cannon—I was SO relieved.

But then she said I could help her, if I wasn't afraid of a little gunpowder. I didn't like the way she smiled when she said that. I saw a hint of my old Evil Twin.

"Yeah, no, thanks," I said. "I'm doing a rap song. I don't need a partner for that."

Except I kind of do. What's a rapper without a backup musician?

If I were still dreaming big, I'd ask Eddy Enderman. He's the coolest kid at school, and all he'd have to do is stand there on stage and my act would take first place, for sure.

But Eddy and I aren't exactly friends. At least, not yet.

I can count my friends on two feet.

There's Sam, of course. And I guess I have to count Ziggy, even though I swore we'd never be friends. He's kind of growing on me—like a mushroom on a log. But I can't picture him rapping. That dude has NO rhythm. Things would have to be pretty bad before I'd ask him.

Who else? Well, there's always Sticky, my loyal pet squid. But squids don't have that many talents. Don't get me wrong—he's pretty cute. And he's stuck by my side through a lot of rough times.

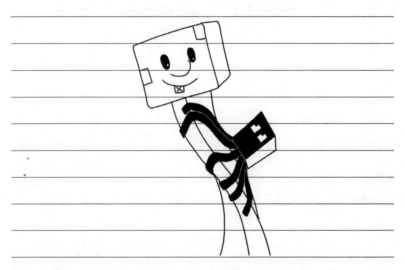

But I don't think Sticky can *help* me up there onstage.

So if I have to do this on my own, I'm going to need to get a grip on my stage fright. But HOW??

Can Willow Witch brew me up a potion of Courage?

I might have to be a whole lot nicer to her from now on.

DAY 2: WEDNESDAY (MORNING)

Okay, so now I'm seriously worried about the talent show.

See, we had music class last night at school. Yeah, you heard me right—MUSIC. Art class turned into music class this month. I guess there aren't enough emeralds in the budget to have both classes, so we have to alternate.

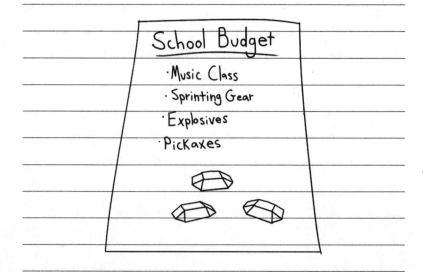

Well, that's okay by me, except our music teacher is the SAME teacher we had for art: Ms. Wanda.

And I really think that crafty witch should stick to
teaching art.

She asked us today who our favorite musicians are.
When I jumped up and said Kid Z, she said, "Kid
who?"

REALLY? How can a music teacher not know the most
famous rapper in the Overworld?

Then she told us she was bringing in "visiting
musicians" to help teach the class. I'm pretty sure
that's just another way of saying, "I don't really
know how to teach this class."

The first thing we were going to learn about was
percussion. And guess who our visiting musician was?

BONES.

Yeah, THAT Bones. The skeleton with the attitude.

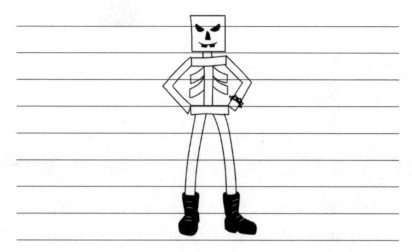

I just about fell out of my chair when I saw *him*.
He came in with a pair of drumsticks and sat down
by the drum set in the corner. And I really, really,
REALLY hate to say this, but he was pretty good.

I tried not to watch—or even listen. But let's face
it, that was a losing battle. Everything in the room
was vibrating to the beat of the drums. My desk.
The floor under my feet. And across the aisle? Sam
the Slime.

That slime was wiggling and jiggling so much, I
thought he was going to slide right out of his seat.

And the whole time, he had this goofy grin on his face. That guy does NOT know how to play it cool.

When Bones was done, people actually clapped, which made me want to throw up. Then, as he walked out of class, he shot me this smirk. I know exactly what he was thinking. It was like I could read the words in a speech bubble above his bony head.

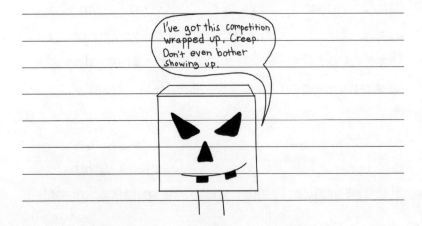

And you know what? He might be right about that. Because at the end of class, Ms. Wanda told us she had good news. SHE was going to be in charge of the talent show.

Great.

I really *hope* she's not the only judge. If she is, Bones is gonna win for sure. And I'll be lucky not to get booed off the stage.

I couldn't get the beat of Bones's drums out of my head after that. During social studies class, I could still hear it—like the way my heart thuds in my ears when I watch a scary movie or get anywhere near a cat.

I could feel the vibrations of those drums, too, like silverfish running across my skin. And I started to itch.

Just in case I didn't mention it yet (and I *probably* didn't, because I really don't like to talk about it), I have this skin thing called psoriasis. It's pronounced SORE-EYE-A-SIS.

It sounds like a deadly disease, I know. But it really just means itchy skin. And sometimes a rash. And you know what makes it worse?

STRESS.

Which I'm feeling a lot of right now.

The other thing that makes it worse is sweating. So by the time I got to sprinting class after school, I was determined not to sweat. I was running so slowly, I was practically walking. I didn't even mind when Ziggy Zombie zoomed by me and left me in his stinky, green dust.

But then I glanced over at the spider riding class in the field next to ours, and the first spider jockey I saw was Bones. He was pretty much galloping across the field on his red-eyed spider. Is there nothing that skeleton can't do?

While I was watching him, I started to think about the talent show again. And I started to sweat. Not the sweating that happens when you run fast, but the sweating that happens when you're sure something bad is going to happen.

I tripped on a shoelace and landed flat on my face. Of course, Bones saw me do it—and about a half dozen of his bony buddies. He shouted, "Jeepers, Creeper. Walk much?"

But after my face-plant, I sat there, thinking and sweating. And that was when it came to me—the perfect way to get out of sprinting class.

I decided to tell Mom that my psoriasis was acting up again because I've been sweating WAY too much in sprinting class. It's genius!

Before I got home this morning, I rolled around in the grass and gave myself a full-body scratch so that she could see the rash. By the time I walked through our front door, my itchy skin was glowing like redstone.

Unfortunately, Mom couldn't see me—or anything else. She was doing yoga, and her body was bent into some weird upside down pose. I could hear her muffled voice calling hello, but I couldn't see her face.

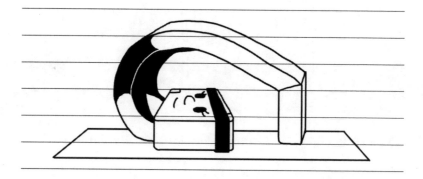

I hung out for a few minutes, but it didn't seem like Mom was getting up anytime soon. (Maybe she was stuck and didn't want to say so.) By then, my skin wasn't so red anymore, so I decided to try again later.

Now my plan is to get a good day's sleep, and when Mom wakes me up to go for our run, I'll hit her with it—the perfect excuse to get out of sprinting.

I can see it now. Mom will feel so bad for making me go to sprinting class that she'll immediately let me quit. And out of guilt and love, she'll probably even make me pork chops and roasted potatoes for dinner.

And I'll have Bones to thank for it.

DAY 2: WEDNESDAY (NIGHT)

Me again. Sorry for the water drips on the page, but I've taken TWO showers since I last wrote. Why?

Well, let me tell you.

I did NOT get out of my nightly run with Mom. And she's WAY faster than Ziggy Zombie, my normal running buddy. My legs are so stiff that I could barely walk to the dinner table.

I was sure Mom would listen to reason when I told her about the psoriasis. But she didn't. She just said I needed to use my coal tar lotion again.

I said I'd BEEN using it, but it wasn't working. I mean, I used plenty of the stuff last month when I was itchy, and it definitely was no miracle cure.

But Mom had an answer for that one, too. She went to the cupboard and pulled out a bottle of something stinky. "Apple cider vinegar," she called it. "After our run, you can dowse yourself in this stuff."

And she held me to that. When we got done with the run, I took a shower, and then she pretty much

gave me ANOTHER shower in apple cider vinegar.
As soon as I sat down at the dinner table, Chloe
scrunched up her nose and said, "Gross, what
stinks?"

The smell was so bad that Cammy started to cry,
which meant she was probably going to explode any
second. And Dad used that as an excuse to leave the
table with her. "I'll eat later," he said—which I think
was code for "after the smelly boy leaves the table."

Cate asked me if I was trying some new cologne. I
couldn't tell if she was joking or not, but since it

was the first time she'd spoken to me all week, I gave her a polite, "No."

And then I ate my pork chop as fast as I could. It was burned to a crisp, just the way I like it. But have you ever noticed that when something smells bad, everything TASTES bad, too? I might as well have been eating vinegar pork chops. Drinking vinegar milk. And topping it all off with a chocolate-vinegar cookie. Blech.

I think we set a record for the fastest Creeper family dinner ever. As soon as it was over, everyone cleared out of the kitchen, and I took another shower.

There's no way I'm wearing this vinegar stuff to school tonight. But it looks like I'll be going to sprinting class, after all.

Again.

DAY 3: THURSDAY

Boy, some mobs are sure touchy. Especially slimes going through caffeine withdrawal.

When we got to school last night, there was this sign on the vending machine that said, "No more caffeinated beverages (at the request of parents)."

Sam didn't really get what that meant at first. He lifted up the sign and looked underneath it. "Where's the hot chocolate?" he asked me, as if I was the one who had taken it out and hidden it somewhere.

By third period, Sam said he had a headache. By lunchtime, he was downright crabby. And that's not a word I've ever used to describe Sam.

He was all quivery, and I could tell he needed to drink SOMETHING. But when he put his emeralds into the vending machine and bought milk, I almost ran for cover.

See, my itchy skin is bad, but Sam has something worse. He's lactose intolerant. That means he can't drink milk. Well, he drinks it, but he shouldn't.

And last night, he did.

I heard his stomach rumbling in music class. It was way louder than the flute our latest "visiting musician" was playing, that's for sure.

By social studies class, it sounded like Sam had a lava pit bubbling up inside him. And by the time we hit science class, I knew he was about to blow.

We were learning about sticky pistons. Our teacher had JUST told us that you craft sticky pistons using slimeballs.

And Sam's gas erupted. Sky high.

When that green cloud filled the room, there was this awkward silence. No one knew what to say—or maybe everyone was just afraid to breathe.

But I had Sam's back, like any best friend would. I cracked a joke. I said, "I guess Sam here is one STINKY piston!"

Well, everyone laughed at that. Except Sam. When the bell rang, he didn't even wait for me. He just grabbed his books and bounced out into the hall.

Sheesh. You do a guy a favor, and that's the thanks you get?

I caught up with him just as some skeleton said, "See you later, Stinky Piston!" He laughed as he walked away, his bones rattling.

Chloe crept up from out of nowhere and wanted to know what the kid was talking about.

Since Sam was still giving me the silent treatment, I explained to Chloe that we'd been learning how to make sticky pistons out of slimeballs. Her eyes lit up, and she said, "Hey, I might need one of those pistons for my talent show project. Sam, can I borrow a slimeball or two?"

Well, I'm not the hissing kind of creeper, but I almost got all hissy on my sister. First of all, why did she need a sticky piston for a cannon? Second, Sam is MY friend. Why was she asking my friend for favors? Third, it was obvious that Sam was in a bad mood, so I thought Chloe should back off.

But before I could say so, Sam's face broke into a wiggly grin, and he said, "Sure!"

Just like that.

I'd been trying to get Sam out of his funk all night, and my Evil Twin managed to do it in about ten seconds flat.

Sam perked up and told me all about his slimeball stash at home. He said it's really paid off for him, because all kinds of kids have been coming to him for slime.

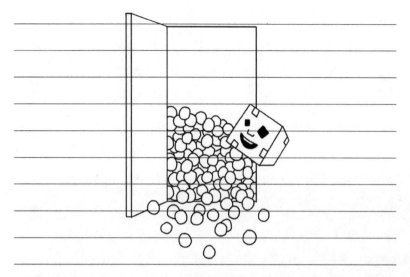

He said Willow wanted slimeballs to make magma cream for her potion of Fire Resistance, so she could walk through fire as part of their talent show act.

"Even one of the spider jockeys wanted to borrow slime!" Sam said, as if that meant he and the jocks were best buds now or something.

I couldn't believe what I was hearing. Sam was helping everyone else with the talent show, even JOCKS. But not me—his best friend! And the way things were going lately, I could really use Sam's help.

So I suggested—and it was only a small suggestion—
that people might be USING Sam to get what they
wanted. I told him I hated to see that happen,
because he was my best friend in the whole
Overworld. And I said that if he still wanted to apply
for the VERY important role of being my backup
musician, I would let him.

He could have at least considered my generous
offer. At least for like a second. But he didn't. He
reminded me that he was helping Willow with her
act. "I told you that already," he snapped.

Well, I didn't think I deserved that kind of attitude.
So I said something else—and I admit, I'm not proud
of this. I asked him if it had OCCURRED to him that
maybe Willow was only with him to get magma cream
for her potions.

"Think about it, Sam," I said. "She's an EIGHTH
grader. She could be going out with a spider jockey
if she wanted to!" That part was true, because
everyone knows that Bones has a crush on Willow.

Someone probably should have cut me off after
the "maybe other people are using you" part.
Maybe before that. Maybe even before the "Stinky
Piston" part. Because Sam was done talking to me
now.

He wiggle-walked away from me as fast as he could.

So now I've got to do some research to find out
how long caffeine withdrawal lasts. Or how to sneak
hot chocolate into Mob Middle School and get it to
Sam on the sly.

I need Mr. Cheerful back. Pronto.

DAY 4: FRIDAY

Witches. I could really live without them.

Willow came up to me at school last night and asked if I'd talked Sam into doing his own talent show act.

Huh? Moi?

The truth was, I never said anything LIKE that. I was trying to talk Sam into helping ME, not into doing his own thing.

But I guess what I said to Sam about Willow using him must have gotten under his skin. When I met up with him in history class, he said he'd decided not to be anybody's assistant. He's doing an act of his own.

He wouldn't tell me what it was exactly, but at lunchtime, there was a sign-up sheet on the wall. We were all supposed to write down what kind of act we'd be doing. Willow, Chloe, and Sam all wrote their acts. And Sam wrote "Trampoline."

TALENT SHOW
Sign-up Sheet

Fire Resistance

Cannon

Trampoline

Bones and his gang of rattlers happened to be standing by the sheet, and Bones was all like, "So you're a real live trampoline now, huh? Should we call you Sam-poline?"

Then another rattler tested Sam's bounciness by lobbing an apple off his head. That apple actually bounced pretty high. It landed on top of the vending machine, where I'm pretty sure it'll stay for the rest of the school year.

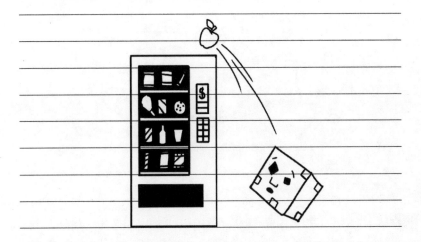

It was all a big joke for Bones and his crew. But here's the thing: Sam on a trampoline is going to be the act to beat. How do I know? Because I've seen him on his trampoline, and he is a bouncing MACHINE.

Sam was so excited about his new act that he let the apple thing bounce—er, roll—right off. He even asked if I wanted to come over for a sleepover to help him build a bigger and better trampoline than the one he already has.

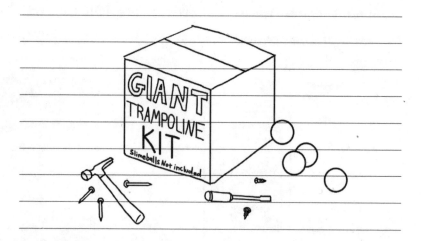

But I shot that idea down right away. I told him I have my OWN act to work on.

I probably could have been a little more supportive. But now Sam's got this great idea for an act, and he'll probably be all done building his trampoline by Monday. Meanwhile, I've got to write a rap song. And come up with music. AND face my stage fright.

Sam didn't seem to notice my mood. In fact, he THANKED me for giving him the idea to do his own act.

"Yeah, okay," I said. "No problem."

But it's definitely a problem. Now I'm going to have to be twice as good onstage, because I don't just have to beat Bones.

Now I have to beat my best friend, too.

DAY 7: MONDAY

I tried to work on my rap song all weekend.

Usually, I can write raps in my sleep. I think them up ALL the time—like when I'm sitting in class, or when Dad's lecturing me, or when Sam is going on and on about how great Willow is.

But when I sat down and tried to work on this one, things kept getting in the way. I mean, I HAD to clean my room. And then I was missing a sock, so

I dug under my bed until I found it. Phew! Then I decided to organize my sock drawer to make sure THAT wouldn't happen again.

I even got up early tonight to work on my rap. And I was making progress, too. I made some pretty good changes, I think.

Itchy
v
~~Itching~~
v
I'm ~~Itchy~~, yeah, I'm Itchy . . .
Itchin' to be free.
You're itchin' to be you and
I'm itchin' to be me.

But then I heard all this music from down the hall. What in the Overworld was going on down there? A party? I had to go investigate. An artist can't work under those kind of conditions.

I found Mom in the living room exercising to another DVD. I was thrilled about that, because I thought it meant we could skip our run before dinner. But Mom said she was just warming up for our run with some Zombie Zumba.

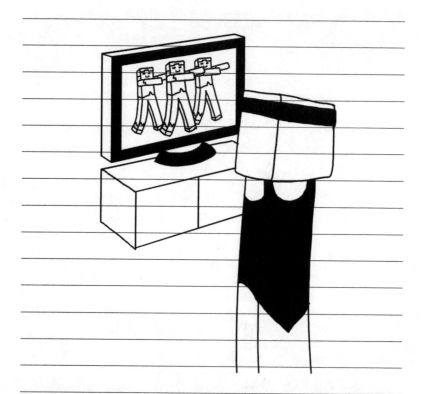

If you ask me, Zombie Zumba is just a bunch of zombies dancing. And like I've said before, zombies aren't exactly known for their rhythm. But the music was pretty catchy. Cammy must have thought so, too, because she kept getting in Mom's way, bopping her little green head to the beat.

"Can you take her?" Mom finally asked, huffing and puffing. "I thought your dad was going to, but he disappeared."

That sounded about right. Dad was a pro at creeping out of baby duty. So I decided to find him. I just followed all the banging noises coming out of the garage.

I went inside, and you know what Dad was doing? Helping Chloe build her cannon! He looked up at me from underneath the black contraption, his guilty face covered in gunpowder.

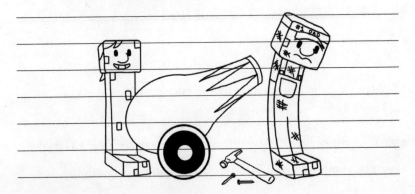

I thought Dad helping Chloe was really unfair, and I told him so. "What about MY project?" I asked.

But when he offered to help me with my rap song, I shut right up. The LAST thing I need is Dad rapping with me at my middle school talent show.

So I stopped complaining to him and went back inside to complain to Mom instead.

She was still working out and didn't want to hear it. "We can talk about it during our run," she said.

Well, going for a run sounded about as fun to me as rapping with Dad. I had to find a way out of it, and fast. Cammy was still tripping Mom up, so I saw the opportunity to make a deal.

I told Mom I'd watch the baby, but that I had a LOT of schoolwork to do. "So if I watch her, I probably won't have time to go running tonight," I said. "Maybe not even tomorrow night. My homework is too important."

Normally, Mom would have seen right through my scheme. But she was too into her zombies and their Zumba. So all she said was, "Dass fly, Ch-Cheryl. (Huff, puff.) Sane Q." (Translation: "That's fine, Gerald. Thank you.")

As I led Cammy away from the living room, I felt pretty proud of myself. I'd just learned a valuable lesson about when to ask Mom for pretty much WHATEVER I wanted.

And all it cost me was a little time with my sweet baby sister. And her seventeen very creepy creeper dolls. They look so real! Some of them hiss and everything.

Cammy's favorite is the one that blows up and has to be put back together. Go figure. When I got tired of sticking that doll's head back on, I hid her under a blanket, hoping Cammy wouldn't notice.

Well, she noticed, all right. Her face turned red and crumpled right up. I knew I had to act fast. I whipped off the blanket to show her where her favorite baby was hiding.

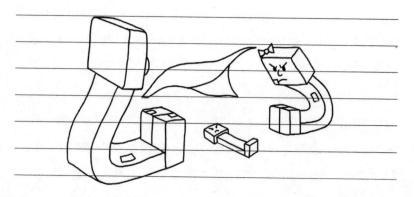

But Cammy was faster. I had just enough time to throw the blanket over my OWN head. (When in crisis, save yourself, I always say.)

The blast rocked the floor beneath me. And when I peeked out from under the blanket, gunpowder drifted down like snowflakes in the Taiga.

Cammy managed to pull herself together. But we were surrounded by a gazillion baby doll heads and legs. Cammy squealed with happiness and started handing me the parts to put back together. I swear, that little creep changes moods as quickly as Sam the Slime!

I held my breath, hoping Mom hadn't heard the blast. If she thought I couldn't handle this babysitting gig, I might have to go running after all.

Luckily, her Zombie Zumba music was pretty loud. But I wasn't going to take any chances on another explosion. I decided to take charge of the situation.

As I stuck a plastic leg into the bottom of a creeper doll, I did what I always do at times like this. I started rapping.

I had Cammy's full attention now. And her dolls', too. As I lined them up in a row, they stared at me, not even blinking. And while I was rapping for those dolls, I didn't have a single bit of stage fright.

"Baby doll, c'mon, baby doll,
Don't go crying, please don't bawl,
Here's four legs and here's your head,
Now, baby doll, it's time for bed."

But as I made up rap after rap, I wondered, "How come these are so easy? And the rap I NEED to write isn't?"

Sometimes life is SO unfair.

DAY 8: TUESDAY

Well, the pressure's on now. I found out at school last night that I have to finish my rap song by Friday. THIS Friday. Why? Because Ms. Wanda broke her foot.

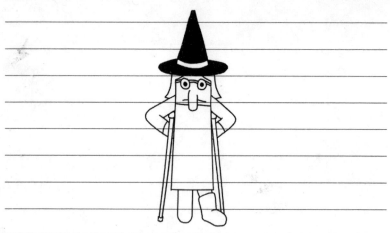

What does her broken foot have to do with my rap song, you ask? That's a very good question. I asked the same thing.

As it turns out, Ms. Wanda won't be able to teach for a while OR help out with the talent show. I thought that might be good news at first. I mean, I'm not glad she broke her foot, but . . . my own feet might have done a happy dance when I learned she wasn't in charge of the talent show anymore.

Then I found out Mr. Zane is taking over.

Maybe now would be a good time to mention that Mr. Zane and I go way back—all the way to September. See, I wasn't always the sprinter I am today. Before sprinting class, I signed up for self-control class. Mr. Zane was the teacher of that particular extracurricular. And even though I think I have very good self-control for a creeper, Mr. Zane didn't think so.

I blame it on Sam. That wiggly slime couldn't sit still during meditation. I'll admit, I might have poked him once or twice. But let's face it, meditation is pretty boring. Can you blame a creeper for trying to make it more fun?

So Mr. Zane looked at the talent show sign-up sheet and decided he needs to review my rap lyrics. By Friday. He wants to make sure they're "appropriate."

I think that's pretty unfair. He didn't ask to see Sam's trampoline act. And I can think of all kinds of ways THAT could be inappropriate, especially if Sam drinks milk the day of the show.

But, no. Mr. Zane singled me out, like I'm some
sneaky creeper. I tried to tell him I hadn't even
written the lyrics yet. And he said, "Well, I guess
you'd better get started, then."

He didn't even care when I told him I already had
something due Friday—my essay for language
arts. We're supposed to write about someone who
inspired us, like a hero or a mentor or something.
That got assigned last night, too, so teachers are
really piling it on right now.

And did I mention my itchiness? By the time the
morning bell rang, I was dying to get out of school
and back home where I could scratch myself silly.

See, I try not to scratch in public—on account of the "Itchy" nickname. But when a creeper has to scratch, he HAS to scratch!

The only problem was, I couldn't go home. Because of sprinting class. Or . . . could I?

There was a voice in my head that said, "Go." That sounded an awful lot like Mom's voice. And then another voice said, "Don't go." I'm pretty sure that one was mine.

So you know what I didn't do?

I didn't go.

I just didn't go.

Instead, I crept off to the Creeper Café. It's pretty close to my house, and it has tall booths so I could hide out there—and even scratch if I had to without being teased about it.

I tried to work on my rap. Mostly, I just waited for time to pass so that I could go home without anyone asking why I was there so early.

I don't know why I even worried about it, though. When I got home, Mom was running laps around the house, pushing Cammy in a stroller. Mom is OBSESSED with this fitness thing. But I guess it helps me out, because it keeps her out of my business.

I heard Chloe banging around in the garage already, so I didn't think she was going to bust me for skipping out on sprinting. She takes strategic explosions class, which is on a field near sprinting class. But she's so into her cannon-building these days, she's probably skipping out on her extracurricular, too. I mean, why work on blowing yourself up when you can blow up a cannon instead?

The one mob who won't stay out of my business is Ziggy Zombie. I'm sure he'll bust me first thing tonight at school, wanting to know why I wasn't on the sprinting field. But I'll deal with that tonight. Right now, I have bigger fish to fry. Like lyrics to write. And an essay due.

X Lyrics

In THREE days.

DAY 9: WEDNESDAY

So last night I sat at the lunch table and just WAITED for Ziggy to ask why I wasn't in sprinting class.

Usually I put Sam in between me and Ziggy at the table. See, Ziggy is the most disgusting eater I know. Food practically LEAPS out of his mouth when he talks. And it's almost always rotten flesh this or rotten flesh that. His mom must have the Rotten Flesh Recipe Book, because I've seen it all.

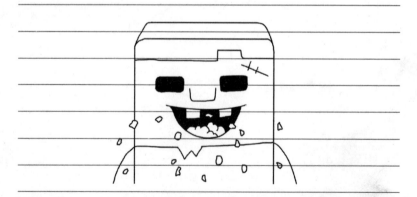

But last night, Sam was sharing a sandwich with Willow at the other end of the table. I guess they made up after the whole "she's just using you for your magma cream" thing.

I was hoping that meant they'd be doing a talent show act together, too—that Sam would give up his trampoline act. That way, I wouldn't have to worry about the slime upstaging me. I even handed Sam a pen so he could cross his name off the sign-up sheet.

But he just stared at the pen, all confused. And then he told me the trampoline act is still on. Rats.

Then he went back to his smoochy sandwich-eating with Willow. I swear I saw them count to three just so they could both take a bite at the same time.

Bones saw it, too, from a nearby table. I could tell from his expression that he enjoys watching them about as much as I do. Which is not much. Especially since he's crushing on Willow.

So he flicked a melon ball at Sam. Bones is a pretty good flicker. I know, because he's flicked a lot of food at me.

Usually I don't appreciate the skeleton's food-flicking skills, but today, I enjoyed watching that melon ball bounce off the back of Sam's head. I mean, he kind of had it coming.

Anyway, back to Ziggy. Without Sam sitting next to me, I felt like a wide-open target.

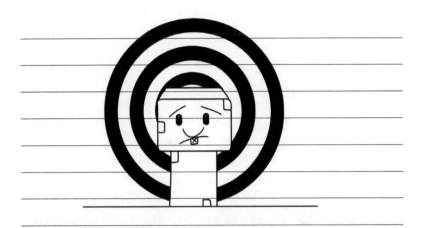

I was just waiting for Ziggy to pounce and bust me for skipping out on our after-school thing. But he didn't.

Instead, he took a big bite of a rotten flesh fajita and asked if HE missed anything in sprinting. Because it turns out, he didn't go either! What are the chances?

I guess my luck is finally turning around. I feel like Fate is telling me that it's okay that I skipped sprinting. In fact, I'm pretty sure it's telling me I SHOULD skip sprinting. And who am I to argue with Fate?

So, after school, instead of heading to the sprinting field, I went straight to Creeper Cafe. I think I'm making progress on my rap song. I copied it onto a fresh sheet of paper, anyway, and I sharpened my pencils so I'll be ready when inspiration strikes.

I'm on a definite roll now. Wish me luck.

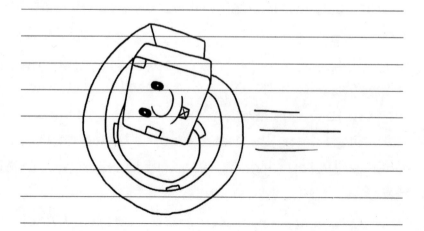

DAY 10: THURSDAY

Last night, Ziggy didn't even wait until lunchtime to bust me. He cornered me at my locker before first period and asked why I missed sprinting.

I could have told him the truth and said I'm just not going to go anymore. But I don't want to let the kid down too hard.

See, I kind of have to stay on the ins with Ziggy. There's a part of me that worries I might need him in the end.

I have to finish this rap song AND find a way to get past my stage fright in the next couple of weeks. If I can't—and I'm just saying IF—I might end up asking Ziggy to be my backup musician. He wouldn't have to dance or play an instrument or anything. He could just hit the "play" button on my laptop.

I'm not that desperate yet. Not even close. But a creeper has to think ahead.

So I made up a fib about sprinting class. I told Ziggy that I sprained my knee bone while I was jogging with my mom.

I know, it doesn't even make sense. But it was the first thing that popped into my head, and I didn't think Ziggy would question it. I mean, he's not the brightest zombie in the pit.

But he DID ask questions. All kinds of them. Like, "Which knee bone?" And, "Can you move it like this?" And, "What about if you go like that?"

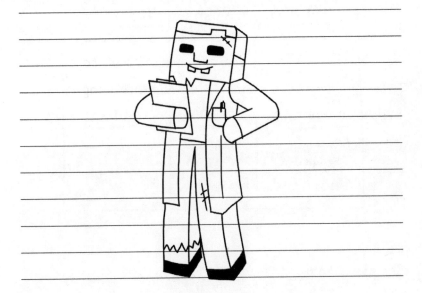

Finally, I had to shut him down. I told him not to worry about my injury, that I'd be back at sprinting class any day now. And then I limped off, trying to remember which "knee bone" I'd sprained so I could pull off the act.

My rap lyrics are due tomorrow. And my essay for language arts. And now I've got a zombie breathing down my neck, watching my every move.

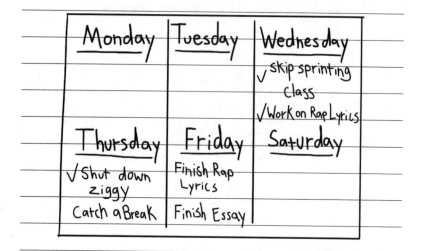

Monday	Tuesday	Wednesday
		√ skip sprinting class
		√ Work on Rap Lyrics
Thursday	**Friday**	**Saturday**
√ Shut down ziggy	Finish Rap Lyrics	
Catch a Break	Finish Essay	

Sheesh. Can't a creeper catch a break?

DAY 11: FRIDAY

Caffeine. I finally get what all the fuss is about!

I stopped at Creeper Café on the way home from school this morning and bought a super-deluxe hot chocolate with whipped cream and sprinkles.

Then, while the rest of my family slept (those lazy bums), I whipped off my rap lyrics AND my language arts essay.

Well, I actually kind of combined them. I figured my rap song was so amazing, it could probably get me a good grade in language arts, too. So I printed two copies of it. I thought that was pretty creative, especially for a sleep-deprived creeper.

Anyway, as soon as I was done, I tried to lie down for a nap. But my eyelids wouldn't shut no matter how hard I tried.

Then Mom popped into my room from out of nowhere and said it was time for our run.

Really? Already? Thank Golem it's Friday and I can rest this weekend.

TGIF

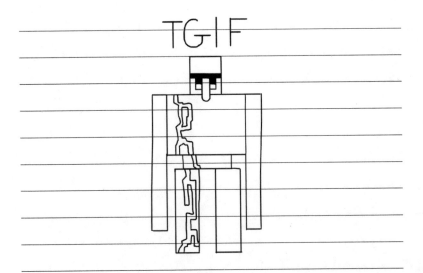

I tried to keep up with Mom, but I swear I was sleep-running. In fact, I ran straight into the stone wall around my neighbor's flower bed—I didn't even see it.

81

I really whacked my knee a good one, too. Ouch! At least now I don't have to fake my limp around Ziggy. I'm limping for real.

I kind of sleep-ate my way through dinner, too. My head kept bobbing, and when I'd snap it back up, I'd catch Dad watching me.

He had this worried expression on his face, like he thought I'd been hanging out with some of the trouble making mobs at school, getting high on spider eyes or poisonous potatoes.

"Dad, I don't do that kind of thing," I said.

"Huh?"

Then I realized he hadn't actually asked the question. So I said I was fine—just tired from staying up all day doing homework.

Well, that was a mistake, because Mom wanted to know why I'd put off my homework till the last minute. She called me a procrastinator. I told her I really didn't appreciate that kind of language.

I told her that, for her information, I hadn't gotten my homework done because I'd been working on my talent show act. And that it was stressing me out. And that I had this stage fright thing going on, and I could really use some support around here.

I know, I was being dramatic. I blame it on the fact that the caffeine was wearing off. Now I know why Sam was so crabby last week.

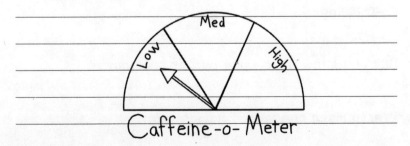

Caffeine-o-Meter

Mom looked like she was going to launch into lecture mode. But Dad, good old Dad, spoke up first. He said he had some great advice for taking care of stage fright.

Well, let me tell you, I was all ears.

For a minute there, I thought Dad was really going to turn things around for me. I was ready to forgive him for helping Chloe with her cannon and everything.

But you know what came out of his mouth?

Pretty much the WORST advice ever.

He said, "Imagine all the mobs in the audience are in their underwear."

Chloe snorted into her mushroom stew. And I looked at Dad like he was a crazy creeper—as if he'd just gotten bitten by a cave spider. I didn't even know how to START responding to advice like that.

So he kept talking. "You know, like picture them without pants on. It'll make you less nervous."

Now Mom was giving Dad a weird look, too. And I'm pretty sure I even saw a smile creep across moody Cate's face.

"Dad," I finally said, "creepers don't wear pants."

He thought about that. Then he cleared his throat and said, "Right. Well I'm pretty sure it was a zombie who gave me that advice."

Figures. If I'd wanted advice from a zombie, I would have just asked Ziggy.

So much for Dad helping me. He should really stick to building cannons.

DAY 12: SATURDAY

So I finally crashed this morning after yesterday's caffeine high. But I sure didn't sleep very well. I kept having weird dreams, one after another. In one ALL of them, I was performing my rap song onstage.

In the first dream, I looked out at the audience and realized it was filled with zombies. "Perfect!" I thought. That meant I could actually use Dad's dumb advice and picture them in their underwear.

But that didn't work, because somehow they KNEW I was picturing them in their underwear. And those half-naked zombies got mad and started pelting me with rotten flesh.

In the next dream, my rap was going pretty well. I had this great beat going, and everyone in the audience was dancing along. I saw Sam wiggling and jiggling, that goofy grin on his face. And then I saw ME sitting next to him. HOA.

So if I was in the audience, who was onstage?

I looked down and realized I was holding drumsticks. I had these long, bony fingers, and I kind of had the urge to flick something with them. My bony hands were attached to these long, bony arms, and . . . ACK! I suddenly realized I had turned into BONES.

In the last dream I was still onstage. But I wasn't at Mob Middle School. I was in the Nether, and there was fire EVERYWHERE. It crept and curled around the stage, getting closer and closer to my feet. I could feel my skin burning and blistering.

When I woke up, I was itching so badly I thought my skin WAS on fire. I whipped on the light and ran into the bathroom for a cold shower.

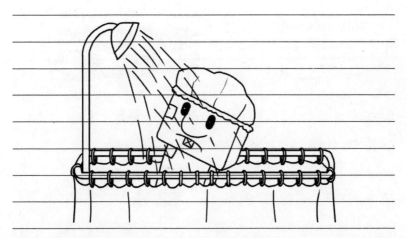

So right then and there, while I was shivering in the shower, I made a decision. Ice-cold water has a way of making everything pretty clear.

I decided it's time to talk to Willow Witch. If I ask her really nicely, I'm hoping she'll brew me up some kind of potion of Confidence.

I don't even know if that's a real thing. But if a witch can make potions that turn people invisible, a potion of Confidence should be a piece of cake.

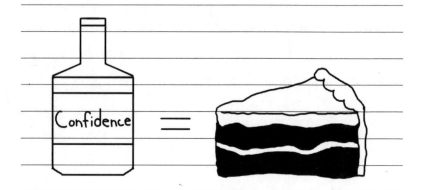

See, I'm pretty sure it's going to take a miracle to get me through this talent show.

Or a little bit of magic.

DAY 15: TUESDAY

Do teachers never take a weekend off?

I got both of my assignments back at school last night—my rap lyrics AND my language arts essay. It's not that I don't appreciate that kind of turnaround time. It's just that I was hoping to coast for a while without having to think about my rap.

See, I really need to move on to a DIFFERENT part of my 30-Day Plan. I need to talk to Willow about this stage fright stuff. I need to find music to go with my lyrics. I need to make a playlist. I need to MOVE ON already.

Anyway, the good news is, Mr. Zane approved my lyrics. He wrote a few nitpicky things, but he didn't find anything "inappropriate." Whoop-dee-do. Call the Creeper Chronicle. Big surprise there.

Gerald J. Creeper
Language Arts

C -

Come See me.

A rap by Gerald Creeper Jr.

I'm Itchy, yeah, I'm Itchy....
Itchin' to be free.
You're itchin' to be you and
I'm itchin' to be me.

Bouncin' like a slime
Or rattling those bones.
Moaning, groaning, teleporting,
Anything goes.

My language arts teacher, on the other hand, wasn't as impressed with my rap as I thought she would be. She said I misunderstood the assignment. Huh.

We were supposed to write about a person we admire, right? And my rap was all about Itchy. That's ME. What's wrong with admiring yourself?

Grown-ups are always telling us to be ourselves, and love ourselves, and blah, bliddy, blah, blah, blah. Then when we actually DO, they swat us down like silverfish.

So I'm thinking maybe my teacher is the one who didn't understand. If she'd read between the lines of my rap, I'm sure she would have seen my genius.

I'm I, yeah, Itchy....
I ___ to be free and
Y_____
I itchin' to be
B_u___n' to be
Or rattling those bones.
Moaning, groaning, teleporting,
Anything goes.

But it's like Ms. Wanda used to say: "Some people just don't appreciate art." So I'm just gonna take the C- and move on.

DAY 16: WEDNESDAY

I finally got the chance to talk to Willow this morning.

Well, first I had a panic attack in science class. One minute I was carefully pouring water out of a test tube into a dish of bubbling lava. We were learning how to make obsidian. No big deal.

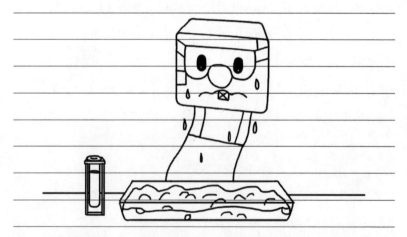

But that hot lava must have reminded me of my dream—the one where I was onstage in the Nether, and the flames were coming for me. Because the next thing I knew, my heart was pounding and I couldn't breathe and sweat was POURING down my

95

face. I couldn't get my safety goggles off fast enough!

Sam looked horrified. It kind of makes me laugh now, picturing his wiggly, worried face. He bounced this way and that, trying to figure out what to do. Finally, he ran to get the teacher, who called the school nurse, who brought me outside.

I have to say, sitting in the moonlight with a cool breeze on my face DID help me feel better. After a minute, I started to think maybe I wasn't going to die. And when the school nurse asked if I'd been worried about anything lately, I almost laughed in his face.

"Yeah," I told him. "Maybe a little worried."

He said that I'd probably just had a panic attack.
Like it was no big deal. Which made me think that
skeleton has never had one himself.

When I finally felt good enough to go back to class,
Sam was being really nice to me. Until I asked him if
he was meeting up with Willow after school.

When I told him I needed to talk to her, he got kind
of weird—especially when I wouldn't tell him what
it was about. Was he JEALOUS or something? Like I
would ever want to date Willow. I could almost toss
my cookies just thinking about it.

The real reason I didn't tell him what I needed to talk to her about is I don't want him to know how freaked out I am about the talent show. See, Sam looks up to me. I'm the calm, cool creeper. He's the one who gets all quivery about stuff.

He already saw me freak out about a dish of lava—I don't know how I'm going to explain that one. But if he overheard me asking Willow for a potion of Confidence, it would turn his whole Overworld upside down. I just don't think I could do that to him.

So I said I had to ask Willow something about the talent show. Finally, he led me to her locker, but then he kind of hung around. He pretended to go to the bathroom, but I could see his green butt sticking out from behind the water fountain.

I lowered my voice and asked Willow if she'd ever brewed a potion of Confidence. I said I might be in the market for something like that if she had the skills to whip it up.

I was hoping she'd jump at the chance, or at least ask me how many emeralds I'd pay for it. But she just said, "Nope. That potion doesn't exist."

Sheesh. Talk about a lack of imagination.

Then I asked if I could get some potion of Invisibility. I KNOW that exists, because she used it last month to spy on Bones.

See, it had just occurred to me that if I were invisible on stage, I might not be so nervous. In fact, if I could get enough of the potion, I could splash it on the whole audience and turn THEM invisible. If I couldn't see them, maybe I wouldn't freak out!

But Willow just narrowed her witchy eyes. "Why do you want it?" she asked.

She sure wasn't making this easy. And I was starting to sweat. Plus, I could see Sam getting antsy. He was going to bounce back over any second now.

So I whispered in Willow's ear. "I have stage fright."

"You have steak fries?" she said, scrunching up her eyebrows. And that girl has REALLY thick eyebrows.

"No!" I said it again. "I have STAGE fright."

This time, she understood. But do you know what she said?

She said she wasn't really feeling inclined to help me with my talent show act. She dragged out the word "i-n-c-l-i-n-e-d" when she said it, the way Mom would have.

Then she reminded me that I had kind of ruined HER talent show act when I talked Sam into dropping out of it.

Wow. And here I thought we were way past that by now. But I guess witches really know how to carry a grudge.

And I guess I'm going to have to figure out another way to stay cool onstage.

DAY 18: FRIDAY

Eddy Enderman never lets me down.

I don't know why I didn't ask him for help in the first place. He's like the King of Cool. If ANYONE can teach me how to keep it together onstage, it's him.

The only problem is, you can't just go up to Eddy and start talking. You kind of have to wait for an invitation—or be brave enough to look him in the eye.

When I first started here at Mob Middle School, Cate warned me to NEVER look an Enderman in the eye. "I mean, like, EVER," she said. "I'm serious."

But if there's anything I've learned since then, it's that my big sister doesn't know everything.

Because one day, I DID look Eddy in the eye. And nothing bad happened. In fact, I learned some things about Eddy. I learned that his real name is Louis. And that he really, really doesn't like rain.

I know, those things aren't going to win me a prize or anything. But I might have a shot at getting some advice from Louis Edward Enderman if I play my cards right.

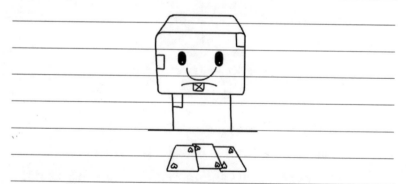

So I finally caught his eye in the cafeteria last night. I stared right at him and tried to send a secret message. "Help! I need some of your coolness! RIGHT NOW!"

No one saw me doing it. Sam was too busy staring dreamily into Willow's eyes over a bowl of mushroom stew. And Ziggy was under the table.

When I bent down to see what he was doing, I saw him pick up a hunk of rotten flesh dog that had fallen out of the bun. He actually scraped it off the floor and popped it back into his mouth. So I was pretty much done eating after that. The perfect time to talk to Eddy.

When Eddy saw me looking his way, he did what Endermen do. He teleported. Right to my table.

And every head in that cafeteria suddenly whipped around to look at me.

What was Eddy Enderman doing talking to a sixth grader? That's what they wanted to know. I could almost hear their brains buzzing, trying to figure it out.

Eddy just ignored them. He said something like, "What's up, Gerald?" He's pretty much the only one here at school who doesn't call me Itchy, which I appreciate.

I didn't really want to talk to him in front of Sam and Ziggy. He must have figured that out, because when I got up and started walking toward the vending machine, he came with me. He's got these long legs, so I had to take like eight steps for every one of his.

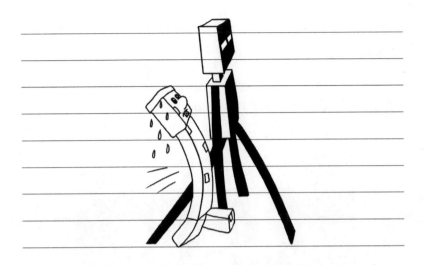

While I sprint-walked to keep up with him, I said,
"Nothing's up. I mean, you know, nothing much. Just
this talent show thing that's got me kind of freaked
out. It's just stage fright. No big deal."

Well, he knew it WAS a big deal. You don't look an
Enderman in the eye if it's not.

So he said, "You have to practice, that's all. Find an
audience. Practice until you're not so freaked out.
Be cool, dude." And then he was gone. I seriously
don't even know where he went.

But I thought about what he'd said. An audience? Where could I find one of those?

I pictured Cammy and her creeper dolls.

I had the PERFECT audience right at home. So when Mom said maybe I should ask my sister to help me with my act, I guess she was right.

I'm going to rehearse ALL weekend. And my Exploding Baby sister (who happens to love my rap music) is going to help me.

DAY 20: SUNDAY

Well, I didn't exactly practice ALL weekend. But I saw my chance tonight. I asked Mom if she wanted to do some of her Zombie Zumba. I figured that would get me out of our before-dinner run, especially if I offered to babysit Cammy.

Mom seemed kind of touched by my offer. I think I scored some big points, actually.

Then I helped Cammy set up all her creeper dolls on her bed. Some of them were missing legs from the last time we played together. So I tried to fix them up. It was kind of fun, actually, figuring out which legs went with which little creeper.

If anyone at school saw me with those dolls, I'd die of embarrassment.

I'd have to build a portal to the Nether and never come back. But a creeper has to do what a creeper has to do. And right now, I have a rap song to practice.

It turns out that my rap goes really well with Zombie Zumba music. Mom had the volume cranked way up, and at first I thought it was going to mess with my act. But when I started rapping, I could do it right along with the music. And Cammy thought that was pretty great.

TOO great, in fact. She laughed. She danced. She made her dolls dance. And then she EXPLODED with happiness.

Did you know baby creepers could do that? Well, I'm here to tell you—they can.

Good thing I have another copy of my rap lyrics, because the one I was reading in Cammy's room was pretty much blown to bits.

But as shredded paper and gunpowder floated down around me, I got an idea—a pretty great idea. FIREWORKS.

I used to make them with my old buddy, Cash
Creeper.

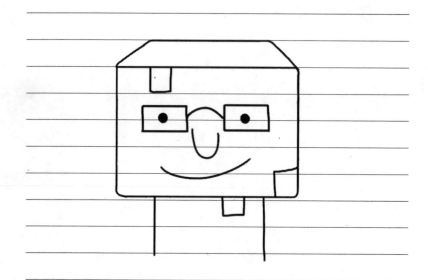

If I could make some more, I could use them at the
end of my talent show act. It would bring the house
down! (Well, not like Cammy did with her explosion,
but the mobs in the audience would be cheering like
CRAZY.)

So I ran out to the garage to find some gunpowder.
We keep it in a big trash bin for emergencies, like
this one. But when I pushed open the garage door,
I could barely fit inside!

Chloe's cannon thing is HUGE. I couldn't even find Dad. When I called for him, he answered, but his voice sounded really far away. Was he INSIDE the thing?

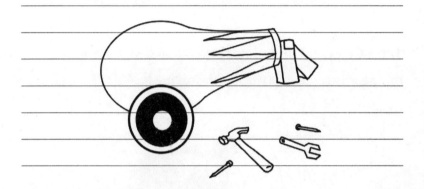

Chloe asked me what I was doing out there, like I was spying on her or something. Like she owns the garage, and I was trespassing.

I told her I was looking for gunpowder, because I was going to use it for my act. And it was going to be really great. But when I said that last part, I didn't even believe it myself. What's so great about fireworks when your sister has a ginormous CANNON?

Then Chloe informed me that there was no more gunpowder. That's right, she used it ALL for her cannon.

When she saw how mad I was, she said in a snotty voice, "I asked if you wanted to help with the cannon, but you said no."

Then she shrugged and went right back to whatever she was doing. When did my Evil Twin learn how to build a cannon, anyway?

I blame Dad. I think it should be illegal for grown-ups to help with middle school projects. Some parents get way too carried away. If she won, he'd probably be right there onstage with her, kissing that trophy like a big, creepy kid.

As I left the garage with no gunpowder, I felt like a creeper who had ZERO chance of winning the talent show.

How do you compete with a slime bouncing on a giant green trampoline? A witch walking through fire? A skeleton with a wicked talent for drums? And your own sister getting shot out of a cannon? I mean, SERIOUSLY?

I'm just a rapper with no props. No potions. No fireworks. And let's face it. The only audience that's ever going to love my act is my baby sister and her dumb baby dolls.

So the only question I have left now is . . . why even bother?

DAY 22: TUESDAY

Why bother? Let me tell you why. Because Mr. Zane said at school last night that there would be a very important guest at the talent show.

Well, THAT changes everything.

I'm losing my mind, trying to figure out who it could be. A talent scout? A reporter from the Creeper Chronicle? A famous rapper? Maybe even (gasp) Kid Z himself??? This really could be my lucky break!

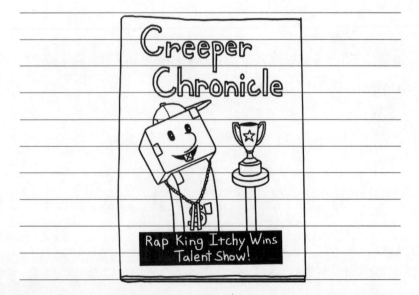

So there's no quitting. I've just gotta find a way to make my act bigger. Better. The BEST.

But I can tell that everyone else feels the same way. Bones has been up to his old tricks lately, getting up in everyone's face. Sam is acting crabby again, and it's got nothing to do with caffeine. I think he and Willow even had a fight the other day, but it sure didn't last long. (Too bad.)

And at home? Chloe and I aren't even speaking. She's acting more and more like the Evil Twin I know and don't love.

But I can't worry about other mobs and their moods right now. It's GO time.

I *have* to pull out all the stops. Turn over every rock. Put every plan in motion, from A to Z. I MIGHT even have to . . .

. . . ask Ziggy to be my backup musician.

I know. It's risky business.

But did I mention there's a lot riding on this talent show now?

So it's Ziggy Zombie's lucky day. I'll ask him tonight at school so we can start rehearsing TOMORROW.

DAY 23: WEDNESDAY

So I chased down Ziggy first thing last night and told him I was about to offer him the chance of a lifetime.

I said that when Kid Z showed up at Mob Middle School and discovered Itchy, a breakout new rapper, ZIGGY would be the zombie onstage behind him. Itchy's sidekick. His right-hand man.

And do you know what that zombie said?

He said NO.

Say WHAT?

He said he wouldn't even BE at the talent show because he'd be getting ready for something called "Halloween."

Ziggy went on and on about it. He said all the villagers walk around outside on October 31. They dress up in different skins and go from door to door, filling up bags with food. And Ziggy and the other zombies stagger around outside, too, moaning and groaning and trying to scare the villagers. It's a zombie thing, he said.

Whatever. I'd heard enough.

I couldn't believe I'd just gotten rejected by Ziggy Zombie. I'm pretty sure that was an all-time low for me.

As if that weren't bad enough, he started in on me again about sprinting class. "Looks like your knee bone is better now," he pointed out.

I guess in all my excitement about the talent show, I've been forgetting to limp.

Well, I told Ziggy my knee bone was definitely NOT better. I even showed him by contorting my body in different ways. "It hurts when I do this," I said. "And this. Oh, and this." I felt like Mom doing her crazy yoga poses, but I had a point to make.

Ow
Ow
Ow

Mr. Zane poked his head out of a classroom and scolded me. "No inappropriate dancing in the hallway, Gerald," he said.

SERIOUSLY? What's WITH this guy?

I wanted to say, "You know what I think is inappropriate, Mr. Zane? A ZOMBIE in charge of a talent show on October 31. Shouldn't you be out scaring villagers or something?"

But I didn't say it. Because, well, you know. That would have been inappropriate.

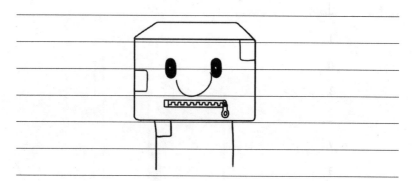

So instead, I stormed off down the hall, making sure to limp this time. My knee bone was definitely acting up again.

So take that, Ziggy Zombie, and your dumb Halloween. I guess I'm just going to have to win this talent show all on my own.

27	28	29	30	31
		Be Cool	Ditch Stage Fright	TALENT SHOW
				Dumb Halloween

DAY 24: THURSDAY

In music class last night, I didn't even want to look at Mr. Zane. I was still mad at him about the "inappropriate dancing" comment. Doesn't a guy recognize a knee bone injury when he sees one?

Anyway, when he said he had news about the talent show, I had to look up. Because I didn't want to miss a word of it.

Mr. Zane said there's something called a "dress rehearsal" on Monday.

That means we can test out our acts onstage, with music and costumes and everything. So he wants us to bring our music on a flash drive by Monday.

MUSIC?

My skin started itching just thinking about it, because I STILL don't have any music lined up for my act.

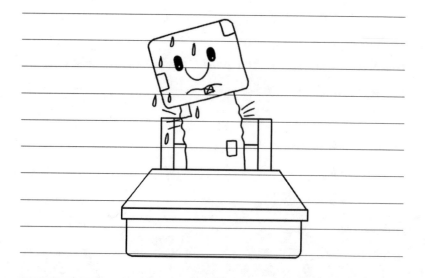

But when I got home this morning, Mom was doing her Zombie Zumba. And then I remembered how her Zumba music went perfectly with my rap.

That's when I had one of my genius ideas. (They've been showing up a lot these days.) I decided that when Mom was done working out, I'd ask her if she could send me the Zombie Zumba playlist. Then I could pretty much check music off my to-do list.

The next thing I had to figure out was a costume. And I knew someone who could help me knock that one off my list, too.

Cate, the Fashion Queen.

I tapped on her door, thinking she wasn't home. But when I stepped into the room, I heard her snoring. She was in bed ALREADY?

I don't get teenagers. They go to bed late and sleep in. Or they go to bed early and then get up in the middle of the day. I stopped trying to figure out Cate a long time ago.

Luckily, she sleeps like a log.

So I tiptoed past her into her walk-in closet. I closed the door and pulled the string to turn on the light. Then I took it all in—all the clothes and the makeup and the wigs.

She even has a mirror in that closet so she can try things on.

Well, I found all KINDS of cool things for my costume, including some chains and a bandanna. I even tried out some of her makeup, which got really messy really fast. Unfortunately, that was right about the time the closet door was flung open.

"What are you DOING in here?" she screamed at me.

It took a while to calm her down. But after I explained what I needed for the talent show, Cate saw her golden opportunity.

See, I don't tell many mobs about this, but Cate used to dress Chloe and me up when I was little. In dresses. Tutus. Feather boas. Wigs. You name it. Even makeup.

I wasn't always loving it then. But NOW? I couldn't think of a better time to let my sister dress me up. If there's one thing Cate knows about, it's fashion.

Now I can check "costume" off my to-do list. And I can tell Mom that I asked ANOTHER sister to help me with my act. Two out of three ain't bad!

DAY 26: SATURDAY

WHOA, what a night.

When I got home from school, I was feeling pretty good about the talent show. I think Chloe was, too. She had this gleam in her eye. Dad, on the other hand, had dark circles under HIS eyes. I think he's been working on that cannon night and day.

Right after dinner, I decided to sneak a peek at the cannon. Dad was already back out there working on it. But Chloe was helping Mom with the dishes, so this was my big opportunity.

But when I got outside, I heard a familiar laugh. A very ANNOYING tinkly-bone kind of laugh. And there was BONES, standing between me and the garage.

I couldn't figure out what he was doing there. Selling Golem Scout cookies?

"Hey, Itchy," he said to me. "What's itchin'?" Then he told me some story about how his cat had run away, and he thought he heard it meowing in our garage.

Well, I would KNOW if a cat were in our garage. I hate cats more than I hate just about anything—except maybe Bones. I can hear a meow from a mile away.

In fact, every time the neighbor's cat, Sir Coughs-a-Lot, hacks up a hairball, I hear that, too. I LISTEN for it. Why? Because I like to know where my enemies are at all times.

And right now, my biggest enemy in the Overworld was trying to get into our garage.

I had a pretty good idea why, too. He wanted to see Chloe's cannon. The thing was legendary. People were whispering about it at school. So I think Bones was worried about losing the talent show to her, just like I was.

Chloe must have had a feeling something was up. She came running out of the house and told Bones that he was not stepping one bony FOOT in our garage.

"Why not, Itchy Witchy?" he asked. He hasn't called her that in a long time, but it fired her right up.

See, Bones knows that Chloe has a short fuse. He can get to her WAY more easily than he gets to me. And he likes to see her blow up.

Usually he does it just for fun. But I had a feeling he had a bigger plan this time. He didn't come all the way out here just to watch a sixth grader blow her top.

"Are you afraid I'll see your cute little creeper cannon?" said Bones. "Aw, I'll bet it hisses just like you, Itchy Witchy."

Sure enough, Chloe started hissing. You'd think a girl who took strategic explosions class would be able to control herself. You'd think she'd know better than to blow up next to the garage. Especially a garage full of gunpowder. And a CANNON.

When I realized what was going to happen, I hollered at Chloe to cool it. But I was too late. I might as well have been trying to control Cammy, the Exploding Baby.

BOOM!

Chloe blew first.

BOOM!!

The cannon blew, knocking me to the ground.

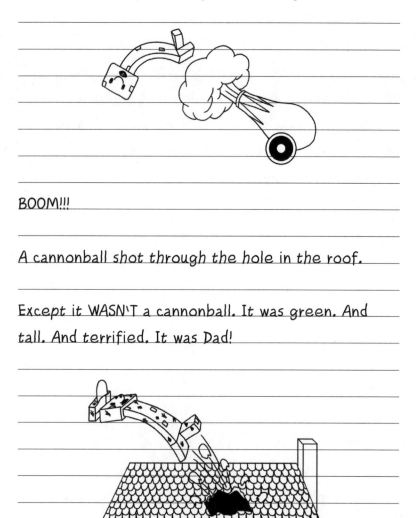

BOOM!!!

A cannonball shot through the hole in the roof.

Except it WASN'T a cannonball. It was green. And
tall. And terrified. It was Dad!

I jumped up and ran after him, as if I could catch him or something. Where's my bouncy friend SAM-poline when I need him?

Luckily, Dad had landed in the apple tree. Upside down. But it looked like he was all in one piece.

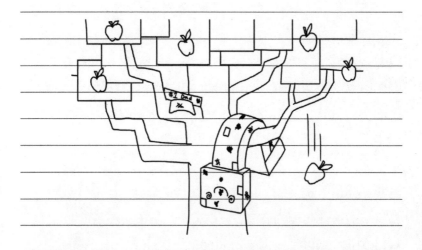

By the time I helped him out and we made it back to the garage—or what was left of the garage—Bones was gone.

And the cannon was gone, too. Blown to smithereens. One of the wheels was spinning around and around in the yard.

Chloe just stood there, staring at where the cannon used to be. She looked so mad, I was afraid she was going to blow up again. Then she started hollering at ME, as it if was all MY fault!

"Why didn't you stand up for me?" she hollered. "You probably WANTED Bones to do that. You're probably HAPPY now because you think you're going to win!"

WHAT?

Okay, maybe I had one selfish thought when I saw all those fresh piles of gunpowder.

But that doesn't mean I'm HAPPY that Chloe's
cannon got blown up. I actually felt sorry for her,
until she turned back into my Evil Twin.

That's when I decided I wasn't going to stand in the
driveway and take that kind of abuse. I still had an
act to prepare for, even if she didn't.

So I snuck out of cleanup duty and back into my
room.

This creeper has to stay focused and keep his eye on the prize. My future as a rapper DEPENDS on it.

DAY 27: SUNDAY

When I woke up this afternoon, I got smart.

I knew that sticking around the house would mean
bad news. Dad would want me to help clean up the
garage. Mom would be on my case again about
inviting Chloe to be a part of my talent show act.

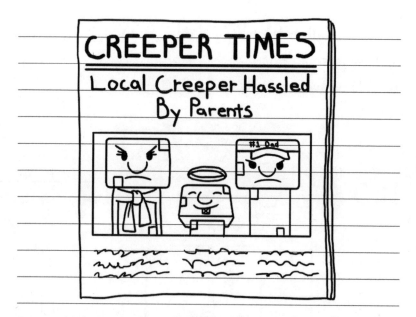

So, somehow, I managed to pull a "Dad" and crept away. And I headed straight toward Sam's house by the swamp.

I wanted to see Sam, but I ALSO wanted to get a look at his huge, new trampoline. See, now that Chloe was out of the talent show, Sam could be my biggest competition. And I had a better shot at winning if I knew what I was dealing with.

But when I got to Sam's, there wasn't a trampoline. Not even a little one. Instead, slimeballs were scattered all over the yard. Had Chloe visited Sam and done some not-very-strategic exploding here, too? What was going ON?

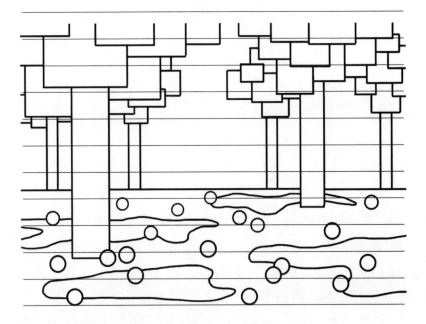

I think I said that out loud, and Sam actually answered me. From up in the air. In a tree.

When I looked up, I screamed. I'm not proud of that, but sitting right next to Sam on the tree limb was his cat, Moo.

Sam thinks Moo and I are great friends, but that slime is mistaken. The one and only time I slept over at Sam's, I woke up with that cat on my head. I still haven't recovered.

Anyway, I tried to ignore the cat and focus on the trampoline. I asked Sam where it was, and he just shrugged. He said he'd broken it all up and donated the slimeballs to charity.

HUH?

"Yeah," he said. "Some spider jockeys came by looking for slimeballs. They said mobs in the Nether need more slime for Fire Resistance potion. Did you know that, Gerald? They asked if I had any to donate. Boy, did they sure come to the right house!"

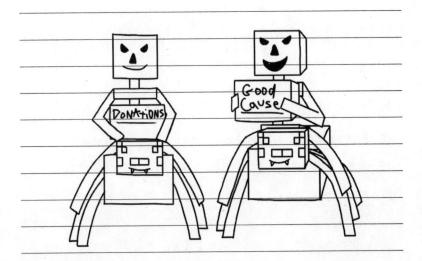

Spider jockeys? Huh, imagine that.

So Bones had struck again. He'd sent his jocks to take advantage of Sam's niceness. Sometimes I think Sam's brain is as mushy as his heart. Good thing he has me looking out for him.

I told Sam that Bones had just pulled a number on him. But instead of getting mad, Sam said he was already working on his next act. And he had his very own assistant.

I shouldn't have asked. But I did.

Next thing you know, Sam was showing me his cat-training act with his personal assistant, Moo. And that act was just about as dumb as it sounds.

I almost said so to Sam. But I didn't want to rain on his cat parade.

Besides, I had my own act to think about. And with Sam's giant trampoline out of the talent show, my act was looking better and better.

As I walked home, I started thinking. If I actually won the talent show, I might have Bones to thank for it. He'd already knocked out two of my toughest competitors.

Defeated

Defeated

But then I started to wonder something else. When was Bones going to come after me and MY act? Wasn't he even a LITTLE worried about it? Was I just small potatoes, or what?

DAY 29: TUESDAY MORNING

I sure didn't have to wait long to find out when Bones was coming for me.

Last night's dress rehearsal was *pretty much the worst* night of my rapping career. I don't even want to write about it, but I have to. Because once I get it down on paper, I can crumple it up and forget about it.

And forget about the talent show.

And forget about becoming a famous rapper.

EVER.

Hopes and Dreams

So here's what happened.

I was on my way to the dress rehearsal. It was
after school this morning, but I had to run home to
change clothes so that Cate could do my makeup.

That meant I had to run BACK to school.

But halfway there, I realized I'd forgotten my
music. In fact, I'd been so focused on my costume,
I'd totally forgotten to make a playlist!

I had no choice—I had to steal Mom's Zombie Zumba DVD. Thank Golem she was running laps around the house instead of working out in the living room.

Anyway, I was running late now because of my second trip back home. So I had to SPRINT all the way to school. And you know how I feel about sprinting.

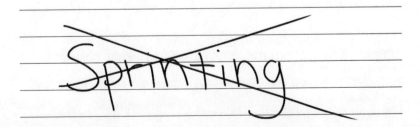

Then I started sweating. When I wiped my forehead, I ended up smearing my makeup. And I started to itch. Badly.

But that wasn't the worst of it.

All of a sudden, from out of nowhere, someone YANKED my backpack and stopped me in my tracks.

When I turned around, there was nobody there! I was dangling by my backpack, which was stuck to the tree, pierced by an arrow. A SKELETON'S arrow.

What happened next was a big, itchy blur.

Bones showed up with his buddies and dumped my backpack. Then Mom's Zombie Zumba DVD—the music for my act—disappeared. I'm pretty sure I'll never see that again.

I could tell you how my dress rehearsal went. But you can probably picture it already. A sweaty creeper with makeup running down his face tries to rap with NO music and a serious case of the itchies.

Complete and total disaster.

That's what I told Willow Witch when I passed her on my way home from school. "You're going to win the talent show for sure," I told her. "Bones ruined everyone else's act. So it's just you and him now."

But Willow said something that shut me right up. She said she wasn't even DOING an act anymore!

"I dropped out weeks ago," she said. "When you convinced Sam to do his own act. My potion-brewing act didn't seem very fun without him."

Well, she might as well have opened up a bottle and splashed a potion of Guilt in my face.

Turns out, Bones wasn't the only one ruining people's acts. I'd ruined one, too.

Mob Middle School
Crime: Talent Show Ruiner
1346533

So, like I said, I'm pretty much done. With everything.

I'm going to take a shower and get this makeup off my itchy skin. Then I'm going to drown myself in apple cider vinegar. And then I'm going to bed.

DAY 29: TUESDAY MORNING (PART 2)

Yeah, so I thought I was going to bed. But I couldn't sleep, even when I tried counting golems.

And sometimes writing in my notebook makes me feel better.

So I was sitting there, looking out the window and thinking about what to write. And do you know what I saw?

MOM.

She was dragging a TIRE around the yard. Chained to her waist. With Cammy riding on it like a sled in the Taiga.

What in the Overworld??? I ran out there to see
what was going on.

Mom said she'd heard that you could use tires for
exercise. She was huffing and puffing, and for the
first time, I saw how STRONG she looked. I mean,
that creeper looked TOUGH pulling that tire. Even if
she WAS my mom!

So I started thinking about how creative she was to
use that tire for exercise. And about how she says

when life hands you moldy mushrooms, you should make mushroom stew.

I'd been handed a lot of moldy mushrooms lately, that's for sure. But Sam and Chloe have, too. And even Willow.

So I decided right then and there that it was time for us all to make a little mushroom stew. Starting now.

Sure, the rest of the creeper world is going to sleep. But I'm wide awake. And I feel like running. No, I feel like SPRINTING. All the way to Sam's house. So that's what I'm going to do.

But first, I've got to go wake up my sister. Yeah, you know which one.

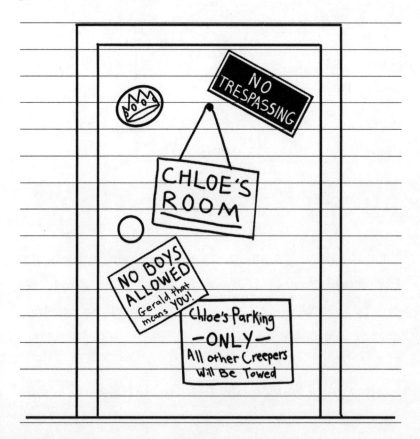

DAY 29: TUESDAY NIGHT

My friends and I worked ALL day on our talent show act. Not the trampoline act or the cannonball act or the walking-through-fire act. No, we came up with something new. Together.

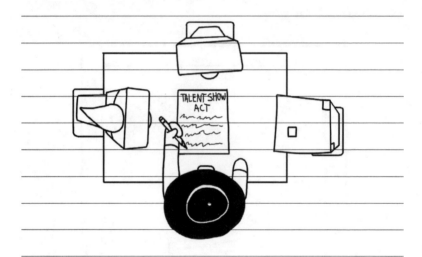

I'm not saying it's any good. I mean, Sam insisted on keeping his assistant, Moo. So there's that. And I'm pretty sure this act isn't going to launch my rapping career anytime soon.

But for some reason, I'm feeling pretty good about it.

Or, at least, I was. Until the doorbell rang right before dinner.

Well, I almost had a panic attack right there in the living room. Ziggy NEVER comes to my house. It was like I knew something bad was going to happen.

And it did.

Before I could step outside with him, he asked if I was ever going back to sprinting class. Because if I wasn't, he wondered if he could borrow my running shoes.

He pointed down at his own, which were full of holes. Boy, that zombie must have been tearing it up on the sprinting field lately.

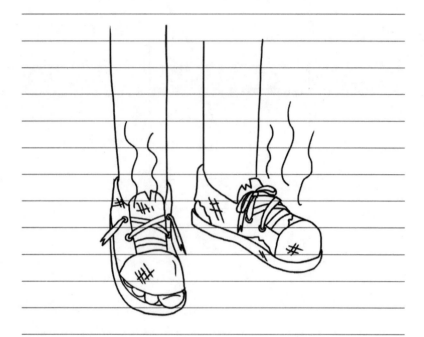

Well, what was I supposed to say to that? My mom was standing right inside the door!

So I did what any sneaky creeper would do. I changed the subject. I told Ziggy I was happy to see him because I'd just put together a new talent show act, and I'd REALLY like him to be a part of it.

I knew he'd say NO. I'd already asked him once. But I figured I'd get points with Mom for being so friendly.

Well, imagine my surprise when Ziggy said YES. And then he invited me to go with him to scare villagers on Halloween night after the show.

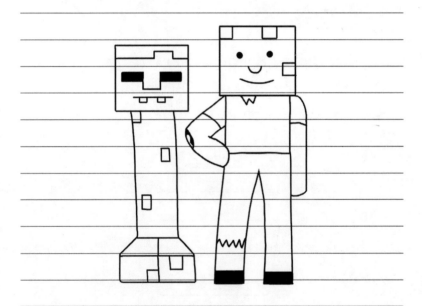

"Halloween?" asked Mom.

Phew! It looked like changing the subject had paid off. But after Ziggy explained what Halloween was all about, Mom snapped right back to attention. She asked Ziggy—NOT me—how long it had been since I'd been at sprinting class.

A smarter kid might have had my back. But, like I've said, Ziggy isn't the brightest zombie in the pit. He told Mom the truth. I hadn't been at sprinting class in three whole weeks.

Well, Mom flipped right out. She said that if I didn't have time for sprinting class, I didn't have time for this talent show either.

I felt another panic attack coming on. But I tried to take a deep breath and think fast.

I figured that Ziggy got me into his mess, so he was going to get me out. I told Mom that Ziggy and my other friends were counting on me. If she punished me, it would hurt them, too.

Dad even backed me up on that. He said maybe we could talk about the sprinting thing AFTER the talent show. So if I hadn't already forgiven him for the cannon thing, I pretty much did right then and there.

So I think the show's still on. Except now I've got to find a way to work a zombie with a big mouth into our act. By tomorrow.

I'm so nervous and itchy, I think I might come right out of my skin. But I have to keep it together. Because what I said to Mom is true.

To Do

~~Become a Famous Rapper~~

Keep it Together

Win Talent Show

Even if I wanted to bail right now, I can't. My friends are counting on me. We're in this together now.

So here goes nothing.

DAY 30: WEDNESDAY

Remember Chloe's cannon?

I feel like I just launched out of that thing and am flying high. I don't think my feet are ever gonna touch the ground.

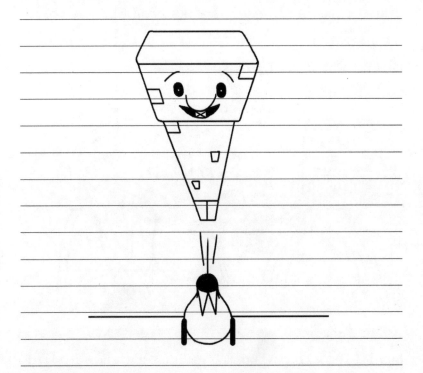

I wasn't feeling that way BEFORE the talent show. No, I was a nervous wreck. But the first act to perform was Bones and his bony brothers. And you'll never guess what song they played.

MY song. Well, it was Mom's song first. Or maybe it belongs to the Zumba-loving zombies.

Yup, Bones stole my music. Sure, he played some drums, too. And there was a skeleton who laid some vocals over the top. And a jockey in the back who mixed it all up on his laptop.

But I'd know that song ANYWHERE. And when I heard it, I was FURIOUS. Like the blowing-up kind of mad, except I'm not that kind of creeper.

When it was our turn to go onstage, I stood up, ready to kick some spider jockey butt.

And to become invisible.

Yup, Willow came through for me, after all. She splashed me with that potion right before we went onstage.

So when I started rapping, I felt cool as a cucumber. I wasn't nervous at all!

I opened the act with a little rap, and when Sam came onstage, I added some new lyrics. They came to me today, just like that. Funny how easy it is to write when you have your friends by your side.

Turns out, Sam's cat-training act was a big hit. He gave commands like, "Moo, don't roll over."

And, of course, she didn't. He tossed one of his slimeballs and said, "Moo, don't fetch." And she didn't.

Well, the audience cracked right up. So Sam started laughing too—so hard that he started bouncing. Which made everyone laugh even more. See, Sam doesn't need a trampoline. His talent is his cheerfulness. He always bounces back, that guy.

Then Chloe came out and did some strategic exploding. She was so good! And when her explosion triggered fireworks—MY fireworks—the crowd went crazy, just like I knew they would.

Willow used one of the fireworks to set her ring on fire, and with her potion of Fire Resistance, she walked right through those flames. I think I'm finally starting to understand what Sam sees in her. She's all right—I mean, for a witch. And a girl.

And Ziggy? Well, it turns out that the guy has rhythm after all. He did *hip-hop* moves while I rapped. I think behind his rotten green flesh, that zombie might be hiding a whole lot of potential.

Getting Ziggy with it

As I was finishing up my rap, I realized something. Mobs in the front row were actually STARING at me. Which would be tough to do if I were still invisible. Which meant . . .

I was no longer invisible.

The potion had worn off! But I didn't even care. My friends and I rapped the last verse together. And then we took a bow.

We're all itchin', itchin,
Itchin' to be free.
You're itchin' to be you and
I'm itchin to be me.

Itchin' itchin'
Itchin' to be free...

So, before I write anything else, I should tell you right here and now that we did NOT win the talent show. Nope. We took second place, and Bones and his band took first.

Now, maybe I would have been upset about that if the show's "very important guest" had actually been a talent scout or a famous rapper like Kid Z. But it wasn't.

You know who the guest of honor was? Ms. Wanda. Our old art teacher with the broken foot.

Bones didn't look all that thrilled when she hobbled onstage to give him his trophy—and a sloppy kiss on his bony cheek.

So after that, I was really okay not winning first place. I felt like a winner anyway. Especially after the show when I happened to walk by Bones and heard him humming a catchy little rap. MY rap, in fact.

Boy, did I bust his bony butt. I smiled wide and said, "Whatcha humming there, Bones?"

I don't even think he knew he'd been doing it. But he shut right up, and his gaping eye sockets got even wider. And then he kind of waved his lame trophy in my face and scurried away.

But I think we both knew who'd won that battle.

So I guess my 30-Day Plan to win the talent show kind of paid off. Not the way I'd planned it exactly. But . . .

. . . maybe even better.

DAY 31: THURSDAY

I didn't think there'd be a Day 31 in this plan, but I have to tell you what's happened since the talent show.

First, I didn't get in trouble for skipping sprinting class. Why? Because when I got home from the talent show, Mom was lying flat on her back on the couch. I guess she overdid it lugging that heavy tire around the other day, and now her back is killing her.

Now don't get me wrong. That's NOT a good thing. But when Dad asked if she wanted to talk about the sprinting class situation, she waved us away and mumbled something about exercise not being "all it's cracked up to be." So maybe I won't get grounded after all. And hopefully Mom won't be looking for her Zombie Zumba DVD anytime soon either.

Then Dad said I could go spook villagers with Ziggy. Chloe, Sam, and Willow came, too. And guess what? We fit right in with those villager kids in their Halloween "skins."

They were dressed like witches, skeletons, and zombies. And I even saw a kid wearing a CREEPER skin like me.

Anyway, this one villager dressed like a witch stopped me and asked what I was "supposed to be." When Ziggy said I was a famous creeper rapper, she looked pretty impressed. She even asked me to autograph her trick-or-treat bag.

When I started my 30-Day Plan a month ago, I thought I'd be so famous right now, witches would be begging for my autograph. So I guess I was kind of right about that!

I mean, I'm not selling T-shirts with my picture on them yet. But, hey, a creeper's gotta start somewhere.